You *are my* Heart

WRITTEN AND ILLUSTRATED BY
Marianne Richmond

sourcebooks
jabberwocky

Published by Sourcebooks Jabberwocky, an imprint of Sourcebooks, Inc.
P.O. Box 4410, Naperville, Illinois 60567-4410
(630) 961-3900
Fax: (630) 961-2168
www.jabberwockykids.com

Library of Congress Cataloging-in-Publication Data

Richmond, Marianne, author, illustrator.
  You are my heart / Marianne Richmond.
      pages cm
  Summary: Illustrations and simple, rhyming text reveal the hopes and dreams of a parent which begin even before a child is born, and are demonstrated through shared giggles, wonderment, grumpiness, and, especially, love.
  [1. Stories in rhyme. 2. Parent and child--Fiction.] I. Title.
  PZ8.3.R433You 2015
  [E]--dc23
                            2014033665

Source of Production: Worzalla, Stevens Point, WI
Date of Production: October 2014
Run Number: 5002652

Printed and bound in the United States of America.
WOZ 10 9 8 7 6 5 4 3 2 1

To my beloved four,
you are my heart.

Before *you* were born,
my heart **always knew**

I wanted to be
a **good parent** to *you*.

I imagined for months
how our family would be,

the things you would **learn,**

the places we'd see.

What I couldn't have known
was **ALL** that you'd be

by *you being you*

and **giving** *to me!*

You are *my* **giggle**

when we make **FUNNY** faces,

blow bubbles,
jump Puddles,

and run
silly races.

You are my **cozy**

when we **snuggle** up tight,

trading KISSES
and WISHES

before our **good night.**

You are
my **wonder**
seeing life
through your eyes,

where boxes
and blankets
are **play**
in disguise.

And you are *my* **brave**
when TOGETHER we face

new things that move us
from our comfortable place.

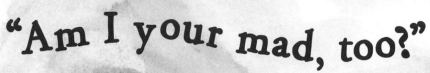

"Am I your mad, too?"

you ask with a smile.

"'Cause I know
you get grumpy
once in a while."

Yes, you are *my* **patience**
that gets put to the test
when the day feels hard

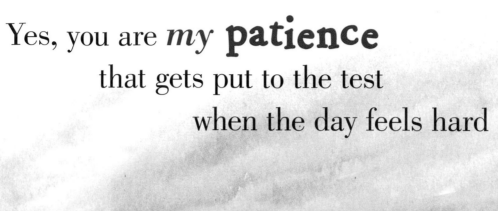

and WE BOTH need a **rest.**

You are also
my **grace**
when we learn
how to say

You are *my* **calm**
when I watch you asleep,
dreaming *your* **dreams**
in your quiet so deep.

You are
my **PROUD**
when your BEST is enough,

knowing trying is TRUE,
and trying is TOUGH.

You're *my*
joy beyond joy
to grow you,
my child,

my
delight

and *my*
thankful,

my
adventure,

my
wild.

You are **ALL** this and more,
a gift from the START.
You are *my* **blessing** and **love**—

ABOUT THE AUTHOR

Beloved author and illustrator Marianne Richmond has touched the lives of millions for nearly two decades through her award-winning books and gift products that offer meaningful ways to connect with the people and moments that matter.